A NOTE TO PARENTS

Reading Aloud with Your Child

Research shows that reading books aloud is the single most valuable support parents can provide in helping children learn to read.

- Be a ham! The more enthusiasm you display, the more your child will enjoy the book.
- Run your finger underneath the words as you read to signal that the print carries the story.
- Leave time for examining the illustrations more closely; encourage your child to find things in the pictures.
- Invite your youngster to join in whenever there's a repeated phrase in the text.
- Link up events in the book with similar events in your child's life.
- If your child asks a question, stop and answer it. The book can be a means to learning more about your child's thoughts.

Listening to Your Child Read Aloud

The support of your attention and praise is absolutely crucial to your child's continuing efforts to learn to read.

- If your child is learning to read and asks for a word, give it immediately so that the meaning of the story is not interrupted. DO NOT ask your child to sound out the word.
- On the other hand, if your child initiates the act of sounding out, don't intervene.
- If your child is reading along and makes what is called a miscue, listen for the sense of the miscue. If the word "road" is substituted for the word "street," for instance, no meaning is lost. Don't stop the reading for a correction.
- If the miscue makes no sense (for example, "horse" for "house"), ask your child to reread the sentence because you're not sure you understand what's just been read.
- Above all else, enjoy your child's growing command of print and make sure you give lots of praise. *You are your child's first teacher — and the most important one. Praise from you is critical for further risk-taking and learning.*

— Priscilla Lynch
Ph.D., New York University
Educational Consultant

To Lucy,
who once was lost
but now is found
—E. R. & D. B.

The artist and the editors would like
to thank Elaine Raphael for her creative help
in the painting of the illustrations.

Text copyright © 1997 by Margo Lundell.
Illustrations copyright © 1997 by Don Bolognese.
All rights reserved. Published by Scholastic Inc.
HELLO READER!, CARTWHEEL BOOKS, and the CARTWHEEL BOOKS logo
are registered trademarks of Scholastic Inc.

Library of Congress Cataloging-in-Publication Data

Lundell, Margo.
    Lad, a dog: Lad is lost / retold by Margo Lundell; based on the book
by Albert Payson Terhune; illustrated by Don Bolognese.
        p.   cm.—(Hello reader! Level 4)
    "Cartwheel books."
    Summary: After being separated from his owners and lost in New York
City, the beloved collie Lad endures such harrowing experiences as being
chased by a police officer, nearly drowning, and being attacked by a vicious
dog.
    ISBN 0-590-92978-X
    1. Dogs—Juvenile fiction. [1. Dogs—Fiction.   2. New York (N.Y.)—
Fiction.] I. Terhune, Albert Payson, 1872–1942. Lad, a dog. II. Bolognese,
Don, ill. III. Title. IV. Series.
PZ10.3.L967Lal   1997
[Fic]—dc20   96-27682
                                                                   CIP
                                                                    AC

10   9   8   7   6   5   4   3   2   1

Printed in the U.S.A.   24

First printing, October 1997

LAD, A DOG

Lad Is Lost

Retold by Margo Lundell

Based on the book by Albert Payson Terhune

Illustrated by Don Bolognese

Hello Reader! — Level 4

SCHOLASTIC INC.
Cartwheel BOOKS®
New York   Toronto   London   Auckland   Sydney

Lad was happy.
The handsome collie was leaving
New York City and going home.
Home was a big place in the country.
Lad and his owners lived in New Jersey,
across the river from the city.
They had come to New York for a dog show.
The purebred collie had won
two blue ribbons.
But the show was huge and noisy.
The master and mistress were sorry they
had dragged Lad to it.
The show had left him dazed and weary.
All Lad wanted was to go home to the fields
and forests he loved.

An attendant stopped them
as they left the building.
"You must put a muzzle on your dog!"
the woman said excitedly.
"It's the law in New York City."

The master headed off to get the car.
The mistress went and bought a muzzle
and strapped it on Lad.
Lad had never worn a muzzle before.
"I'm so sorry, Laddie," the mistress said.
"I'll take it off as soon as we are out
of the city."

The master pulled up in the car.
"Let Lad have the back seat to himself,"
the master told the mistress.
"The poor fellow needs to stretch out."
The mistress opened the car door,
and Lad jumped in.
But the tired collie did not settle down.
The heavy metal muzzle upset him.
It hurt his tender nose.
It hurt his pride.
Lad trusted the mistress with all his heart.
Why was she making him so unhappy?

It was early evening.
The car headed into heavy traffic.
The noises and smells made Lad dizzy.
The pain of the muzzle confused him.
Lad whined, but no one heard him.
He twisted and turned.
He tried to rub the muzzle off.
Finally, Lad stood up on the slippery seat.
He pressed the muzzle against some
metal on one of the doors.
He worked and worked
to pry the muzzle loose.

Just then the traffic cleared,
and the master dashed forward.
He raced the car past a small truck.
Then he made a sharp right turn.
The turn threw Lad off his feet.
The big dog fell against one of the doors.
The sudden weight was too much,
and the door burst open.
Lad fell out of the speeding car
onto the hard, grimy street.

Lad landed on his side.
The breath was knocked out of him.
The delivery truck that the master
had passed was coming right at him.
HONK! HONK!
Lad scrambled to his feet
and sprang to the edge of the road.
The truck missed him by inches.

The master and mistress drove on in the car.
They had no idea what had happened.
The traffic took all their attention.
Finally the mistress turned around
to see how Lad was doing.
"He's gone!" she cried. "Lad's gone!"

Lad stood on the sidewalk staring
at the cars driving by.
The loud honking and car fumes
made him feel sick.
He was frightened.
Lad sniffed the air again and again.

He ran back and forth.
He studied each person he passed.
He was searching for the master
and mistress.
Surely they would come back.

Lad gave up his search at last.
He could smell land and trees nearby.
In fact, it was New York's Central Park.
Lad jumped over a low wall and found
himself inside the park.
The tired collie lay down on the cold
February grass and panted.

At last, the big dog stood up.
He was very thirsty.
Lad had to find water.
He came to a lake in the park
and tried to drink.
The muzzle made it painfully hard.
Lad finally lapped up enough water
to keep going.

What should Lad do next?
He was tired and in pain.
But he did not think of these things.
Lad thought about the Place instead—
about the big house,
about the master and mistress,
about safety and kindness.
Lad's eyes began to shine.
He stood up and took deep breaths.
He turned around slowly.
Suddenly Lad knew where to go.
He lowered his head and trotted westward.
He was heading for New Jersey.
He was heading for home.

CLICKETY CLACK. CLICKETY CLACK.
A subway train rattled by over Lad's head.
He had left Central Park and was crossing
a busy avenue.
He was still traveling west.
He dodged a trolley and reached
the far side of the street.

"Hi, doggie!"
A tiny child on the sidewalk saw Lad
and ran to him.
The child's mother did not notice.
The little one threw her arms around Lad.
He wagged his tail happily.

Suddenly the mother yelled, "Bad dog!"
She yanked her child away and hit Lad
with the package she was carrying.
Lad remembered his training.
He did not strike back.
But he showed his teeth and growled.
The woman screamed.
A policeman appeared and asked
the woman what was wrong.

By then Lad had trotted off
and was halfway down the block.
The woman pointed to him.
"That's a mad dog!" she cried.
"He tried to bite me!"

The policeman chased Lad.
He believed Lad was a dangerous dog.
He knew only one way to stop him.
The policeman pulled out his gun
and fired as he ran.
The bullet missed.

Several boys saw what was happening
and joined the chase.
"Mad dog!" they cried. "Get him!"
Suddenly everyone believed that Lad
was dangerous.
The policeman fired at him again.

Lad felt a hot pain along his left side.
The bullet had grazed him,
but the hurt collie did not stop.
He raced west across two more avenues
and full speed down a hill.
Ahead was the Hudson River.
On the other side was New Jersey.

Lad ran onto a pier that reached out
into the river.
The howling crowd followed.
"There he goes!" they shouted.
"Get him!"
Lad stopped at the end of the pier.
The crowd was coming closer.

Lad looked at the huge river.
He saw only one way to get across.
There was no time to lose.
With one jump, he was in the air.
Then Lad hit the cold, black water
and sank far below the surface.
He struggled back to the top.
When his beautiful head appeared,
the crowd on the pier threw stones
and bits of wood.
"He'll drown for sure!" someone shouted.

Lad swam hard.
The water pulled him
this way and that.
Heavy pieces of wood banged
against him in the dark.
He swam for more than an hour.
His body and mind grew numb.

TOOOOT! TOOOOT!
A tugboat nearly ran Lad down.
Then the swirling water from the tug
almost drowned him.
He held his breath until his lungs
were ready to burst.
The big collie was fighting for his life.

Then it was over.
Lad swam the final yards and felt rocks
and sand under his feet.
With his last bit of strength,
he crawled ashore.
He lay down on a narrow strip of sand.

A long time went by.
Lad did nothing but pant.
Every inch of his shaggy body
was tired.
Little by little, Lad's strength
and breath came back.

At last, Lad could move.
Slowly, slowly he climbed up the tall cliffs
along the shore.
At the top, the weary creature stood
and sniffed the air.
Then he started west again.
His walk was tired and clumsy.
Lad passed through town after town.
Thirst made him feel faint.
The muzzle still hurt.

Finally Lad came to a broken-down
house on a dark road.
A nasty watchdog waited for him
in the shadows.

GRRRRRRR!
The watchdog rushed
out of nowhere and attacked Lad.
Lad tried to open his jaws
to protect himself.
The muzzle stopped him.
Lad was helpless.

Even so, he fought back.
He snarled and whirled around.
He reared up and rolled in the dirt.
The enemy bit into Lad's thick fur
again and again.
Lad jerked loose each time.

Once again the watchdog rushed
at Lad's throat.
This time he found a good hold.
His jaws held more than just fur.
They were gripping a leather strap.
It was the strap that held Lad's muzzle
in place.

Lad pulled away with all his might.
Suddenly the leather strap broke.
The muzzle slid off Lad's nose.
It hung from the jaws of the attacker.
In seconds, Lad was on his feet.
Excitement swept over him.

Lad's old power rushed back.
He attacked fiercely.
The other dog howled in pain.
A man in the house finally stuck his head
out the window.
"You there!" he shouted at Lad.
"Get away from here!"
The man's beaten dog ran off.
Lad let him go and trotted on his way.
He searched for water and found a brook.
The thirsty animal drank
for a full ten minutes.

Then Lad jogged on through the dark.
He was going home!

Dawn was coming.
The master and mistress finally
drove back to the Place.
They had stayed in the city all night
looking for Lad.
They hadn't given up hope,
but the two of them were very worried.

Lad stood on the porch of the big house.
He heard a car coming up the driveway.
He barked in case it was strangers.
Then he ran stiffly to see who was there.
His eyes and nose quickly told him.
His master and mistress had come back.

The mistress jumped out of the car
even before it stopped.
Then she was on her knees,
hugging Lad in her arms.

Lad was covered in dirt and blood,
but the mistress didn't care.
"Oh, Lad!" she sobbed. "Laddie!"
Lad forgot his pain and hurt.
He licked the dear face bending near.
Nothing else mattered.
They were together at last.

— *About Lad* —

The famous collie lived with the
talented animal and nature writer,
Albert Payson Terhune, and his wife,
in Pompton Lakes, New Jersey. The
"Place" was a wooded estate called
Sunnybank.

A series of magazine stories about Lad
were published during World War I.
The stories were very popular. After the
war, the stories were published in a book.
The book about Lad sold very well.
The brave, loyal dog became so popular
that people would drive to Sunnybank
uninvited "to see where Lad lived."
The author was finally forced to put
up gates and keep them closed.

Terhune went on to write stories about
other dogs, but he was always best
known for the tales he told about the
collie. There was no other dog like Lad.
The author said it well in his dedication
to the book:

This book is dedicated

to the memory of

LAD

thoroughbred in body and soul